OTHER
BY PATRICIA .... WILL ENJOY:

THE KIDS OF THE POLK STREET SCHOOL

THE BEAST IN MS. ROONEY'S ROOM
THE CANDY CORN CONTEST
LAZY LIONS, LUCKY LAMBS
IN THE DINOSAUR'S PAW
PURPLE CLIMBING DAYS
and more

THE NEW KIDS AT THE POLK STREET SCHOOL

WATCH OUT! MAN-EATING SNAKE
FANCY FEET
ALL ABOUT STACY
B-E-S-T FRIENDS
SPECTACULAR STONE SOUP
STACY SAYS GOOD-BYE

YEARLING BOOKS/YOUNG YEARLINGS/YEARLING CLASSICS are designed especially to entertain and enlighten young people. Patricia Reilly Giff, consultant to this series, received her bachelor's degree from Marymount College and a master's degree in history from St. John's University. She holds a Professional Diploma in Reading and a Doctorate of Humane Letters from Hofstra University. She was a teacher and reading consultant for many years, and is the author of numerous books for young readers.

For a complete listing of all Yearling titles, write to
Dell Readers Service, P.O. Box 1045,
South Holland, IL 60473.

THE RED, WHITE, AND BLUE VALENTINE

Patricia Reilly Giff

Illustrated by
Emily Arnold McCully

A YOUNG YEARLING BOOK

Published by
DELL PUBLISHING
a division of
Bantam Doubleday Dell Publishing Group, Inc.
666 Fifth Avenue
New York, New York 10103

ISBN: 0-440-40768-0

Printed in the United States of America

February 1993

10 9 8 7 6 5 4 3 2 1

To Mary Cash,
with love

♪ CHAPTER 1 ♪

"**A**nyone there?" Willie Roberts poked his head into the kitchen.

No one. Good.

His mother hated it when he took her stuff to practice drumming.

He grabbed three pots from the cabinet.

Outside, something crashed.

He took a quick look out the window.

His brother, Darrell, was standing on top of a ladder, painting the toolshed.

1

He said he was going to live in it next summer.

He was going to bring out his hamster, Mary Beth, and his goldfish, Jake.

He said Willie could come too.

Willie shook his head. He wouldn't sleep out there in the dark for a hundred dollars.

He watched Darrell reach out to dip his brush into a paint can. Darrell was crazy to paint with snow all over.

The ladder started to wobble.

Willie banged on the window. "Watch out." Too late.

The ladder slid gently down the side of the toolshed. Darrell slid with it.

Willie closed his eyes.

When he opened them, Darrell was dusting snow off his jeans.

Darrell's jeans had paint all over them.

So did the toolshed: yellow and blue paint stripes.

They were the only colors Darrell could find in the garage.

Willie began to open the rest of the kitchen cabinets.

He rooted around until he had found a bunch of things: an old eggbeater, a glass measuring cup, a box of sugar toasties.

He grabbed a milk container out of the refrigerator. Two drops of milk were left.

He slurped them up, then piled the empty container with everything else.

He took them upstairs to his room.

His and Darrell's.

They had stacked a pile of cartons down the center of the room for privacy.

You could hardly see over the top.

Willie lined his kitchen things up on the floor, and sat down in front of them.

At the same time a whirring noise came from behind Darrell's side of the cartons.

It was Darrell's hamster, Mary Beth.

Mary Beth was racing around on her wheel, a hundred miles an hour.

The wheel scratched and squeaked.

Willie hated the sound of it.

He wondered if Darrell's fish hated it too.

He tiptoed around the cartons to look.

Mary Beth looked at him too.

Mary Beth's cage looked wild.

Darrell had painted mountains, and grass, and a huge sun on a piece of paper. He had pasted it on the back of her cage.

"Mary Beth thinks she's rich," he had said. "She's living in a great spot."

Willie dropped Darrell's pajamas over Mary Beth's cage.

Maybe he wouldn't hear the squeak that way.

Willie picked up his drumsticks. He played one on the milk container and the other on the cereal box.

He grabbed his speller, and played a couple of ruffs on that too.

He loved drumming . . . drumming in the Lincoln Lions Band with a real drum.

He began to tap out "God Bless America."

His little sister, Janell, had been singing that since she learned it in kindergarten.

He could feel the beat of it, could hear the words in his head. He pounded the sticks on his dresser, the floor, the cereal box.

He closed his eyes as he played.

He tried a ruff, a paradiddle.

He was on a stage. The audience was roaring, clapping . . .

Whooof.

Something landed on top of him.

Cartons crashed into each other.

"Help," he yelled. "Murder."

"Fight for your life," yelled Darrell.

"You're finished." Willie banged the milk container on Darrell's head.

From downstairs, his mother yelled, "Break something and you're both finished."

Willie lay there laughing.

He watched Darrell roll away from him.

"Hey," Darrell said suddenly. "Hey."

Willie sat up. "What?"

"How come Mary Beth is covered up?"

"I just—"

"What are you trying to do . . . smother Mary Beth?"

Willie rubbed his shoulder. It was starting to hurt where Darrell had tackled him.

Darrell started toward him. "How could you do that to Mary Beth?"

Willie scrambled out the bedroom door. He raced for the stairs.

Chrissie Tripp was on her way up. "While you're in here fooling around, it's snowing outside," she said. "You're wasting time when we should be sledding."

Willie leaned over to see out the front door.

Chrissie was right. Fat white flakes were drifting down on top of last week's snow.

"Go ahead without me," he started to say.

Then he remembered. They had cracked her sled against a tree last month.

"I don't know where my sled is," he said.

"You do so. It's in the garage."

She dashed downstairs ahead of him.

Upstairs, Willie could hear Mary Beth squeaking.

Maybe he should go back and tell Darrell he was sorry. Maybe he should—

"Willie," Chrissie yelled.

He sighed. Then he started down the stairs after her.

♪ CHAPTER 2 ♩

Willie slid along the ice on his driveway. "The garage is a mess," he told Chrissie. "You couldn't find an elephant in there."

"Don't worry." Chrissie slid along next to him. "We'll find your sled."

He pushed up the garage doors. "See?"

"Yecchs," Chrissie said. "You're right."

Willie looked around. There wasn't an

9

inch of space anywhere. Tools and boxes were piled around a rusty old car.

His mother was always fooling with the car.

All it did was cough a little. It never ran.

His mother said she was going to get it going someday. Then they were going to ride in it all the way to New York City.

Willie hopped up on the back of the car to see better.

After a moment he saw the edge of the sled, hidden under a pile of wood.

"It's here. I don't believe it."

Chrissie edged into the garage.

"We just have to move Darrell's stuff." Willie shook off his father's gloves. They were huge old leather ones.

They were great gloves . . . great for drumming his fingers inside.

"If you keep moving like a snail," Chrissie said, "it'll be too late to take a sled ride."

Willie shook his head. He began to drag the boards off the sled.

A splinter tore into his thumb.

"Yeow." He gritted his teeth together. Next thing she'd be calling him a baby.

He pulled off the last board and dragged out the sled. He could feel the sting of the splinter.

"All right," Chrissie said, "let's go." She picked up the rope and started down the driveway.

Willie yanked out the splinter and pulled his hands into the gloves. Then he took a leap and belly flopped onto the sled.

He wondered what Darrell was doing.

He let Chrissie pull him on the sled, pushing with his hands to move it along faster.

In five minutes they were at the college bridge. His father's bridge, the bridge he had spent the winter building. It curved high over the river, glinting silver in the late afternoon.

Ahead of him, Chrissie raised one hand. "T. K. Meaney's up there."

Willie could see someone on the bridge. Someone with a blue plaid scarf.

It was hard to get a good look though. Willie's eyes were watering from the cold. He swiped at his face with the gloves, and started up on the bridge.

His father had loved building it.

If Willie closed his eyes, he could see his father, a bunch of papers under his arm, pointing up, telling the workers where to put the beams, how to . . .

The boy in the scarf turned.

Yes. It *was* T. K. Meaney, grinning, nose running.

"Good. You've got a sled." T.K. raised one shoulder in the air. "Can't find mine."

Chrissie stuck out her chin. "You think

three are going to fit on this? You think I dragged this out of Willie's garage just to—"

"Turns. We'll take turns." T.K. held out his hands. "Me first."

"No, me," Chrissie said.

Willie opened his mouth. Before he could say anything, she was racing down the other side of the bridge.

She charged down the hill toward the college.

Willie stopped at the end of the bridge. He stretched his neck up to look at the top.

His father was right. It was beautiful.

He leaned over the edge to see where it met the frozen river beneath.

His glove dropped over the side.

He ran along the bridge, then down the snowy bank to cross the ice.

As he picked up the glove he saw something . . . something he'd never have seen

if he hadn't been right there, right at that spot.

His mouth felt dry.

He could feel the wind pushing at his back.

Then Chrissie was next to him.

She leaned over his shoulder. "Darrell's been here."

"No," said Willie.

"That's his paint. Yellow."

"No," Willie said again. He could feel a lump in his throat.

"What kind of a mark is that anyway? Looks like a *D* with a hook on one side." Chrissie turned her head to see better. "Maybe a sea gull underneath."

Willie kept shaking his head.

An ugly paint stain snaked across the bottom of the bridge piling.

Darrell's paint.

Darrell's mark.

♪ CHAPTER 3 ♩

It was Monday night, practice night for the Lincoln Lions Band.

In the gym, the fifes sounded first. Jing, jing, jing. Jing, jing, jing.

Willie waited. He watched Jessica, the junior band leader.

Jessica raised her baton.

Willie raised his drumsticks.

Down went the baton.

Willie's drumsticks came down too . . . a rum-pum-pum. He rolled the sticks a little, clicking his teeth, nodding his head.

"Jingle bells . . . jingle bells . . ."

He could feel the beat of it in every part of him. Even his toes kept time.

He didn't have to close his eyes to see the White House. The President had just given him a medal. "Incredible drumming," the President was saying.

Willie looked up.

His father had come into the gym. He was sitting on the bleachers. Willie could see he was trying not to smile.

It was February. Christmas had been over for a long time. No one sang "Jingle Bells" anymore.

It was a good thing his father had missed "Santa Claus Is Coming to Town." They had played that first.

"Per-fec-to," said Professor Thurman when they were finished.

For a minute Willie felt a lump of worry in his chest. Why was his father there?

The professor began to speak. "Great news. It's almost Valentine's Day."

Willie snorted under his breath.

He was sick of Valentine's Day already.

Janell had been cutting out hearts and pasting them all over the place for days.

He had glue on his shoes, on his pants, on his bedspread.

"We're hiring a bus," said the professor. "We're going to Simson City next weekend."

Simson City had the greatest mall. Darrell had gotten Mary Beth there with his Christmas money last year.

Willie swallowed. How could Darrell have done that to his father's bridge?

Maybe if they weren't still fighting, Willie might have asked.

But Darrell had brought more boxes. They reached almost to the ceiling. And Willie wasn't going to be the first one to make up . . . not after looking at that bridge.

The professor cleared his throat. "We're going to compete in a Valentine's Day music contest. We'll win a couple of prizes. Money prizes. Prizes for singing. Prizes for . . ."

He stopped to smile at the fifers. "Prizes for tootling. Prizes for drumming."

Willie's father was smiling now.

Willie knew what he was thinking. Willie was going to win something.

Willie took another look at his father. He had on his good tan leather jacket. A plaid scarf was looped around his neck.

Willie felt a lump in his chest.

Traveling clothes.

"Who's ready to compete?" the professor asked.

Everyone yelled. Willie's father clapped.

Edwin pounded on the drum.

The professor said a few more things, then Jessica blew her whistle. "Baaaa-nd," she yelled. "Disssss-missed."

Willie followed everyone along to the music room. He grabbed his jacket.

Back in the gym his father was waiting. "Thought I'd give you a lift home," he said.

Willie nodded. He could see a small spot of Darrell's yellow paint on his father's sleeve.

Chrissie Tripp came running toward them. Willie knew she was looking for a ride.

He pretended he didn't see her.

He wanted to be alone with his father.

He wanted to hear that he wasn't leaving.

"How about a lift?" Chrissie asked.

"Sure," said Mr. Roberts. "Why not?"

They went out to the car together, their feet crunching on the snow.

Willie's father must have known he was

worried. Just before they reached the car, he gave his son a rough hug.

Chrissie talked all the way home.

"I'd love to win a prize," she said.

"You have to try," said Willie's father. "Do the best you can . . . even if you think you can't win. That's the way."

Willie wished it were last month.

He wished his father had just come home to build the bridge.

Just before they dropped Chrissie off, she leaned over. "Does your father know what Darrell did?" she whispered.

He shook his head as she opened the door and dashed up her path.

"What was she saying?" His father grinned. He thought Chrissie was great.

Willie bit down on his lip, thinking about Chrissie, thinking about the paint stain on the bridge, thinking about his father leaving.

He watched the corner as the car turned.

"I had a call—" his father began.

"Stay home," Willie broke in.

"It's only a couple of weeks. A bridge needs work in New York City."

Willie could feel the tears stinging his eyes. "Why do you always have to . . . ?"

His father put his hand on his shoulder. "I'm always trying to build the best bridge." He grinned. "And Mom's always trying to get that old car to run."

He pulled to a stop in front of the house. "I said good-bye to Mom, and Darrell, and Janell."

Willie looked at the path, the steps bright under the light.

"I'm glad I had a chance to listen to you play," his father was saying. "I know you're going to win a prize."

He reached out to hug Willie again.

Willie hugged him back, then opened the car door, and started up the path.

Behind him, his father rolled down the window. "Take care of your mom, and Janell."

Willie nodded.

"And Darrell."

"Darrell?" Willie repeated. "Darrell?"

But the car had begun to move.

Darrell. Darrell was a year older. And if his father knew that Darrell had painted on the bridge, he'd feel terrible.

Willie stood there in the cold for another minute, feeling the wind against his face and neck.

He'd win a prize for his father.

He'd try really hard.

He went up the steps and into the house.

♪ CHAPTER 4 ♪

"**I** have a plan," Chrissie said the next day in the schoolyard.

"What plan?" Willie asked.

The bell rang.

"Tell you later."

Before he could say anything, she rushed across the yard ahead of him.

He didn't catch up with her until they reached the hall. "Tell me now."

"I'm going to do you a favor," she said.

"What are you talking about?"

"Yes," said Mrs. Lovejoy from the doorway. "What are you talking about when you're supposed to be in the classroom, getting ready to start the day?"

He marched inside.

He hung his coat on the hook next to T.K.'s.

Willie wondered where his father was now.

His mother said he was going to drive all night, and part of today.

He closed his eyes for a second. He had just finished playing "Drum Mania" on the drums. He was winning the prize. His father was . . .

"Reading," said Mrs. Lovejoy.

He pulled out his book.

Everyone was supposed to work on a favorite subject book.

Too bad his book wasn't so hot.

It was all about horses. He loved horses. But these horses didn't do much of anything. They just wandered around the plains and ate grass.

A note landed on his desk.

Meet U in the orditorium.

He looked up. Chrissie was nodding.

Mrs. Lovejoy was somewhere in the back of the room, reading.

Willie made believe he was scratching his foot.

He turned around.

Mrs. Lovejoy looked up.

Willie leaned over his horses again.

He watched Chrissie walk to the front.

He waited until she was out the door, then he stood up.

"Is this really necessary?" Mrs. Lovejoy asked.

Willie looked as desperate as he could.

"I have to . . ."

"Go ahead," she said.

He hurried down the hall.

Chrissie was in the auditorium, halfway to the stage.

"We're going to talk about you," she said over her shoulder. "Right now I've decided I'm going to be your manager."

Willie heard a noise in back of him. He spun around. Nothing.

"Don't get so antsy," she said. "Mrs. Lovejoy's reading a mystery book. The principal's out in the schoolyard."

Willie sank into an end seat.

He ducked his chin down on his chest so he'd be hard to spot from the door.

Chrissie came down the aisle. She sat in a seat in front of him. "Now . . ."

The door opened.

Chrissie dived for the floor.

Willie dived too.

They could see the custodian's feet and legs as he went down the aisle and out the door near the stage.

"Talk," Willie said. "Talk fast."

"I'm talking. I'm talking." Chrissie leaned against the back of the chair. "You're the best drummer in the Lincoln Lions Band."

Willie tried not to smile.

"I want to show you something," she went on.

"We'd better get back." He looked around. "Any minute . . ."

Chrissie put her hands on her hips. "There you go again, Willie. Wasting time."

Willie took a deep breath and sighed.

"You forget something, Willie? You forget I'm your manager? You forget we're going to win a prize?"

"*We're* going to win a prize? I thought I was going to win."

"Well," she said. "Me too. I'll show you."

29

She marched up the aisle and opened the doors.

Willie followed her down the hall.

Darrell was out of his classroom too.

He was standing at the drinking fountain.

"Wait a minute," he said when he saw Willie.

Willie stood in the middle of the hall.

He knew Darrell was going to make up.

He took a step forward.

Then he remembered. Darrell didn't care one bit about his father's bridge.

Darrell didn't care one bit about anything.

Willie started after Chrissie. When he looked back, Darrell was gone.

Chrissie stopped in front of the principal's office.

Willie could see inside. Mrs. DiNardio wasn't sitting at her desk.

He wondered how Chrissie knew Mrs.

DiNardio was outside. He shook his head. That Chrissie was so nosy, she knew everything.

And right now she was staring up. Staring at the ceiling, the lights . . .

She stood there for a second, then raced back down the hall.

"What was that all about?" he asked, as they flung open the auditorium doors.

"The picture," she said. "Didn't you even look? I was nearly expelled for nothing?"

Willie tried to think. The only picture he could remember on the wall was one of Abraham Lincoln.

"Not Abraham Lincoln," Chrissie said.

"Of course not."

Chrissie beamed at him. "See what I mean? We're going to Simson City for Valentine's Day. But it's George Washington's birthday too. Don't you see?"

"No."

"You are slow, Willie. Slow. Think about the Revolutionary War. Think about that picture."

"The picture," he said slowly. "You mean the picture of those two drummers?"

"And the fifer," Chrissie said. "And the guy with the flag in back."

Willie watched her waving her arms around.

Chrissie leaned forward. "We'll get dressed up. I'll stick a bandage on my forehead. You can play the drums. I'll do the fife. We'll win the prize. I just know it."

"Two drummers," he said. "Two."

"So what?" She twirled around laughing. "We'll just have one. No one will know the difference."

"Wait a minute," he said.

Before he could say anything else, Chrissie was at the auditorium door, heading back to the classroom.

33

"No," he said. "I'm not going to do it."

Chrissie looked back at him.

He shook his head. "Uh-uh."

"You're some friend," Chrissie said.

"Listen. I want to win a prize for my father."

"You will. I'm telling you."

"No." He followed her down the hall. Neither of them said a word.

He sat down in his seat.

He wished Chrissie hadn't looked so sad.

He wished he had gone to the bathroom while he was out. He'd have to wait now for the rest of the morning.

♪ CHAPTER 5 ♩

It was Wednesday, suppertime.

Willie was the last one downstairs.

No one was sitting at the table. They never did when his father was away.

Janell was eating in front of the TV in the living room. Her doll, Angelina, was propped up next to her.

Darrell was sitting on the kitchen windowsill, talking with their mother. "If I had one more stripe on that toolshed—red or orange—it would be spectacular."

He stopped talking when he saw Willie.

Willie sank down on the kitchen floor. He leaned against the radiator.

It was warm on his back, cozy.

"Your plate's on the table." His mother smiled at him over her shoulder. She was sitting on a stool with a bandage on her hand. She had hurt it working on the car.

With her other hand she was writing numbers on the smooth white front of the refrigerator. "A little wiggly," she said. "I'm not used to writing lefty."

Willie looked at his mother's writing. His mother loved numbers. She taught math up at the college.

"Formulas," she called the numbers. "They're soothing. They always work out just right."

Numbers didn't always work out just right for Willie.

He had gotten NEEDS TO WORK HARDER on his last three subtraction tests.

He reached up for his dinner plate.

"Fritters?" he said. "Corn fritters? You know I can't stand them. You know they make me vom . . ."

His mother held up her hand. "Don't even think of finishing that word."

She looked as if she were going to laugh though.

She hated corn fritters as much as he did.

He put a tiny bit in his mouth.

Terrible.

He broke the fritter in half. He slid one of the halves under the radiator.

"Here, ant. Here, ant," he said under his breath.

He looked up at Darrell.

Darrell was staring out the window. Every

once in a while he'd take a piece of fritter, stuff it in his mouth, chew, and swallow.

Darrell wasn't paying one bit of attention to food.

Willie wondered what he was looking at.

It was pitch-black outside. Besides, most of the window was covered with Janell's messy red Valentine hearts.

Willie slid his other fritter half under the radiator.

It was getting full under there.

Janell had hidden four pieces of cheese last week.

Darrell had shoved in a slab of nut bread his grandmother had baked.

Now Darrell grabbed his jacket from the chair. "Going outside for a minute."

"It's freezing out there," their mother said. She smiled a little. "Never mind. It's almost Valentine's Day. Soon it will be spring." She looked back at the refrigerator.

Willie knew she was thinking about his father coming back.

He thought about winning a prize. He could see himself calling his father. His father would be really happy.

Then he thought about Chrissie. Chrissie wanting to try for a prize.

Darrell opened the back door.

A gust of wind swept in.

"Angelina is going to get the flu," Janell said.

"She's all right. Don't worry." Darrell pulled the door shut behind him.

Darrell was great to Janell.

Willie thought maybe he should go out after him. Ask him about the bridge.

Willie stood up. He went into the dining room.

He had shoved his jacket in there somewhere.

He went through the kitchen again, shrugging on his jacket. "Be right back."

"Did you eat your—"

"Yes."

It wasn't a lie. He had eaten some of it.

He opened the back door.

He couldn't even see Darrell outside.

"Will-ieeee," Janell whined. "It's freezing."

He shut the door behind him.

He hunched his neck into his jacket collar.

It really was freezing.

The snow was crusty. Long, thick icicles hung from the top of the toolshed.

Darrell must be in there.

Yes, he could hear him singing.

Singing?

He had never heard Darrell sing in his life.

Willie tiptoed across the yard.

His voice was low and gravelly. Terrible.

"I'm a lone-suuuuuum cow-booooy," Darrell moaned.

41

Willie was dying to laugh.

Old Darrell, singing.

Darrell was terrible at music. He hadn't even lasted in the band for two practices.

Willie covered his mouth.

He crept up to the blanket that was Darrell's door and angled his head around to see better.

Darrell was just sitting there in the freezing cold, wrapped in his mother's white lace curtain.

Willie took a step back.

He fell over a board.

Darrell came barreling outside. "I'm going to kill you, Willie," he yelled. "Sneaking up on me. Trying to . . ."

Willie scrambled backward through the snow. He managed to get to his feet.

He raced into the house.

♪ CHAPTER 6 ♪

It was warm on Saturday. Willie headed for the college road.

There was something he wanted to do.

A few minutes later, he stood at one end of the bridge.

For a moment, he stopped to watch the icicles melting in the sun. He broke off a long, spiky one and let the cold water drip into his mouth.

He leaned over to take a look at the yellow paint mark Darrell had made.

He could see the *D*.

D for Darrell.

There were other marks in a circle around the *D*.

Willie wished he could figure out what they were.

A hook?

A bird?

He had been thinking about the mark all day.

It was because of a dream he had had.

A dream about Darrell.

It was something about Darrell painting the bridge.

It was something about Darrell singing.

He woke up wishing they were friends again.

He had looked between the cardboard

boxes, but Darrell was up already, downstairs having breakfast.

Willie dropped the end of the icicle off the end of the bridge. He watched it splinter on the ice below.

Darrell wasn't painting his toolshed now.

He had left it half finished with stripes of yellow and blue in between the gray boards.

He spent all his extra time now inside, singing cowboy songs.

Behind Willie, there was a shuffling sound.

Before he could turn, a voice moaned, "Yeoooooooo."

Willie spun around.

It was Chrissie Tripp.

"What's the matter with you?" he said. "Want me to fall off this bridge? Want me to—"

T. K. Meaney popped up in back of

Chrissie. He was laughing. "You should see your face."

Willie grinned a little.

He didn't feel like smiling though.

He felt like giving Chrissie a good clip in the mouth.

"I've been looking for you," Chrissie told him.

T.K. started toward the other end of the bridge. He sliced icicles off the railing as he ran.

"I didn't bring my sled," Willie said. "Besides, half the snow is gone."

"Not about the sled." Chrissie took a quick look toward T.K. "It's about the Simson City Valentine's Day competition."

Willie thought about his drumming.

He was going to play "Drum Mania."

He had practiced it about a thousand times.

"What about Simson City?" he asked.

Chrissie held her hand up to her mouth. "T.K. wants to win a prize," she whispered.

An icicle dropped from above. It crashed onto the bridge.

Willie jumped back.

"But we need help," Chrissie said. "T.K. and me."

Willie shook his head.

"It would be perfect for Washington's Birthday. You'll drum, I'll fife, and T.K. can just make believe he's . . ."

Willie kept shaking his head.

"No one will know. T.K. will practice almost hitting the drum. But just not quite . . ."

"You're crazy, Chrissie."

"We'd win a prize," Chrissie said. "I know it. T.K. would feel wonderful. I'd feel . . ."

Willie watched T.K.

T.K. was sliding across the ice under the bridge.

He could see Darrell—Darrell's ears any-way.

Darrell had a cowboy hat pulled way down, covering most of his head.

"We're going to win," Chrissie said. "You know it."

Willie swallowed. His father would probably call late tonight.

They could tell him his two sons were the worst in the whole competition.

Next to the bus a car horn beeped. Toot-a-toot toot.

It was probably someone going to the competition.

Willie swiped at the window. All he could see were lights whizzing past.

A few minutes later, the bus pulled to a stop in front of the Simson City Mall.

"Come on," Chrissie yelled.

She and T.K. raced down the aisle.

The professor was yelling, "Take it easy."

Willie took it easy.

He was the last one off the bus.

Heads bobbed along in front of him. Chrissie was wearing a handkerchief around her head like a bandage . . . just like in the Revolutionary War picture. Kenny Bender swung his bugle over his head.

And Darrell.

Darrell looked like an idiot in his cowboy hat.

It looked as if Darrell was really happy though.

It looked as if Darrell thought he was going to win.

Willie felt a lump in his throat. Somehow, Darrell's losing was worse than his losing.

For a moment all he could think of were the good things about Darrell. Darrell taking care of Mary Beth. Darrell teaching him to swim last summer. Darrell crashing over the boxes to wrestle with him.

He missed Darrell.

What about the bridge? he asked himself.

He was sick of thinking about the bridge.

After this was over, he was going to ask Darrell about it.

And no matter what Darrell said, he was going to say, "How about being friends again?"

Maybe they'd even paint over the mark together.

Willie hurried to catch up.

The mall was crowded. He kept hoping he'd spot his mother and Janell. Maybe someone had given them a ride. They didn't seem to be there though.

He held his drum in front of him, trying not to bang into people.

A little boy reached up and gave the drum a tap.

Then he looked at Willie.

He probably thought there was something wrong with him, wearing that white shirt in the middle of winter, and that ridiculous hat.

"It's a costume," he told the boy.

The boy darted away after his mother.

At the end of the mall, a stage was set up.

Blue curtains were tacked on the bottom. A microphone hummed in front.

The contest had already started.

Four girls were doing a song with glasses.

They kept wetting their fingers and twirling them over the glasses.

Sounds were coming out. Sounds that hurt his ears.

Chrissie leaned over toward him. She was trying not to laugh. "They should have stayed home."

Willie nodded.

He played the drums in his head.

"Yankee Doodle went to London . . . riding on a . . ."

The drumbeat changed. "I'm a looone . . ." roll the drums, roll the drums . . . "soooooome" . . . roll the drums . . . "cowboy" . . . two ruffs.

He stopped playing.

He waited while a bunch of kids tried out. Kenny Bender played reveille. It sounded as if his bugle were cracked.

Another girl played the bugle too. She was better than Kenny. Much better.

Then Darrell.

It was a surprise to hear him with someone playing music in the background.

Darrell's voice was smooth and deep.

Except in the middle, when Darrell stopped singing. Stopped and stood there as if he were thinking. Smiling a little. Then beginning again, and ending on a low note that didn't sound quite right.

Darrell sat down as if he were pleased with himself.

He didn't even seem to notice that he had kept the audience waiting while he was standing there still as a stone.

After a while, Willie got tired of listening.

Nine or ten kids were ahead of him, singing or playing.

Then it was his turn. His and Chrissie's and T. K. Meaney's.

For the first time he spotted his mother and Janell in the audience. His mother seemed to have a spot on one cheek. He wondered what it was.

He wondered how they had gotten there.

He marched up to the stage, playing softly.

Everyone quieted down.

Chrissie started in on the fife.

She had practiced at home for hours.

The sound was sweet and high. "Yankee Doodle . . ."

T.K. was tapping the drum, hardly making a sound.

Everything seemed to be going well.

Then T.K. tripped over a rope. His drumsticks clattered onto the stage.

"Shoo," he whispered under his breath.

The microphone picked it up.

It was as if he had shouted it.

He and Chrissie began to giggle.

People in the audience were giggling too.

T.K. was making little gulping noises.

Chrissie was laughing too hard to play.

It ended up that Willie played alone.

He was never going to speak to Chrissie or T.K. again. Never. Not even if he lived to be one hundred.

On the way back to his seat he kept his head down.

The master of ceremonies stepped forward. "I think that's all," he said.

"No," Darrell said. "There's one more."

♪ CHAPTER 9 ♪

The car rattled and coughed.

Sometimes it seemed as if it wouldn't make the hills. It did though.

It kept moving along, moving toward New York City. Moving toward his father.

Willie couldn't stop smiling.

He was sitting in the backseat with Darrell.

It was dark outside, and cold.

Inside was warm. Almost too warm.

His mother didn't know how to turn off the heater.

Up front, Janell was singing. His mother was making believe she was the drummer.

They sounded a little like "Drum Mania."

Willie leaned over and gave Darrell a punch. Then he sat back to think about what had happened.

"My brother's going to play," Darrell had told the master of ceremonies.

"No good," someone yelled. "He had a chance."

"Not like that," said Darrell. "Not solo. Other stuff."

The master of ceremonies nodded. "Why not?"

Darrell began to gather things together: an empty soda can, a Cracker Jack box, an orange juice container, a bottle.

Chrissie stood up to help. She asked a

woman for a pot she had bought in the mall.

Willie just stood there, watching. His mouth was dry.

The end of the stage was two jumps away. He could clear the end. Run, keep running . . .

Darrell and Chrissie were lining everything up.

"What's the name of all this . . . ?" The master of ceremonies waved his arms.

Willie cleared his throat. "Um . . ."

"It's going to be 'Drum Mania,' " said Chrissie. She looked at Darrell. "Right?"

The master of ceremonies looked at Willie.

"I guess so," said Willie.

He sat on the floor with his drumsticks. His hands felt sticky.

He tapped the sticks, one at a time. First on the pot. Then the can. Then the bottle.

The bottle didn't make much noise.

He tapped it louder.

Then he started to play.

At first he played softly.

People stopped paying attention. They began to talk a little, to move around.

The master of ceremonies moved the microphone closer.

Willie picked up the beat a little.

He began to hear the music in his head.

It moved down to his fingers, to his feet.

He tried a ruff . . . a paradiddle.

People weren't talking anymore. They were listening.

In front, the professor began to nod his head, to tap his feet.

Willie forgot about the audience. He forgot about Darrell and Chrissie, about Janell and his mother.

He tapped the sticks against the floor and the sides of the metal chairs.

The master of ceremonies turned the microphone louder still.

A moment later, the audience was clapping in time with the beat.

When he stopped, someone shouted, "More."

He started up again, playing the parts that sounded right, that felt good.

When it was over, the audience clapped for a long time.

Willie didn't look up. He went back to his seat, head down, embarrassed.

It wasn't until later, in the parking lot, holding the envelope with the prize money, that he told himself he had won.

Janell was jumping around. "No bus," she yelled. "We're not even going home."

His mother was grinning. Willie could see that the mark on her face wasn't a cut. It was a small smudge of dirt.

She was grinning, squeezing his arm.

"Wonderful," she kept saying. "We're bringing the prize right to New York City so that Daddy can see it."

They crossed the parking lot and stopped in front of the old red car.

"I did it," his mother said. "Got the thing started for the first time in years."

"Angelina and me in front," Janell said. "It's only fair."

He and Darrell grinned at each other and slid into the backseat.

Willie cleared his throat. "You were good," he told Darrell. "Your voice is—"

"Not bad," Darrell said. "But I don't care about winning. I just needed the money."

"I'll share," Willie began, holding out the envelope.

Darrell shook his head. "I don't need it. I just wanted it for paint. Wanted to finish up my toolshed with another stripe."

Janell leaned over the seat. "We're going to stay out there next summer. Remember?"

"I was right in the middle of the song," Darrell said. "Then I realized. All I had to do was mix the paint together. Take the blue . . . take the yellow . . ."

"Green," said Willie. "A green stripe."

"Dumbest thing, I didn't think of it." Darrell shook his head. "One thing I wasn't dumb about—I knew you were the best. I knew you had to play."

Willie looked out the window.

The bridge.

"How come . . ." he began and stopped. "How come you painted on Dad's bridge?"

"A painter," Darrell said. "Dad said that I'm a painter, and you're a drummer."

Willie nodded. He had never thought about Darrell being an artist.

"Dad and I even worked out a signature." Darrell grinned. "*D* for me. A *J* hook for

71

Janell, and a W for you. All together. It looks nice."

"You painted it on the bridge."

Darrell nodded. "Dad and me. Low down, so no one would see it. Dad said the bridge was his work of art."

Willie started to laugh. He felt like crying too.

Everything had worked out just right.

He picked up his drumsticks and began to play on the backseat. Dum-de-dum. On the metal tray. Rat-tat-tat.

"You're giving Angelina a headache," said Janell. "Enough drumming now."

Willie put his drumsticks on the floor.

The car was moving fast now, going toward his father.

He put his head back against the seat.

He closed his eyes.

He listened to the sound of the drums in his head.